Hello, Family Members,

Learning to read is one of the most important accomplishments of early childhood. **Hello Reader!** books are designed to help children become skilled readers who like to read. Beginning readers learn to read by remembering frequently used words like "the," "is," and "and"; by using phonics skills to decode new words; and by interpreting picture and text clues. These books provide both the stories children enjoy and the structure they need to read fluently and independently. Here are suggestions for helping your child *before*, *during*, and *after* reading:

Before
- Look at the cover and pictures and have your child predict what the story is about.
- Read the story to your child.
- Encourage your child to chime in with familiar words and phrases.
- Echo read with your child by reading a line first and having your child read it after you do.

During
- Have your child think about a word he or she does not recognize right away. Provide hints such as "Let's see if we know the sounds" and "Have we read other words like this one?"
- Encourage your child to use phonics skills to sound out new words.
- Provide the word for your child when more assistance is needed so that he or she does not struggle and the experience of reading with you is a positive one.
- Encourage your child to have fun by reading with a lot of expression . . . like an actor!

After
- Have your child keep lists of interesting and favorite words.
- Encourage your child to read the books over and over again. Have him or her read to brothers, sisters, grandparents, and even teddy bears. Repeated readings develop confidence in young readers.
- Talk about the stories. Ask and answer questions. Share ideas about the funniest and most interesting characters and events in the stories.

I do hope that you and your child enjoy this book.

—Francie Alexander
Reading Specialist,
Scholastic's Learning Ventures

For Adam, who never gives up
—L. G.

To my Grandparents, Frank and Marion
—H. B.

Text copyright © 1999 by Laura Geringer.
Illustrations copyright © 1999 by Holly Berry.
All rights reserved. Published by Scholastic Inc.
SCHOLASTIC, HELLO READER!, CARTWHEEL BOOKS and associated logos
are trademarks and/or registered trademarks of Scholastic Inc.

Library of Congress Cataloging-in-Publication Data
Geringer, Laura.
    The stubborn pumpkin / by Laura Geringer; illustrated by Holly Berry.
        p.   cm. — (Hello reader! Level 3)
    Summary: A cumulative tale in which a farmer, his wife, his daughter,
his cow, his dog, and his cat can't pull the enormous pumpkin off its vine
until they are helped by a tiny mouse.
    ISBN 0-590-10850-6
    [1. Folklore.] I. Berry, Holly, ill. II. Title. III. Series.
PZ8.1.G352Pu   1999
398.22 — dc21
[E]   97-47299
                                                                      CIP
                                                                       AC
10 9 8 7 6 5 4 3 2   9/9 0/0 01 02 03

                        Printed in the U.S.A.   24
                    First printing, September 1999

by Laura Geringer
Illustrated by Holly Berry

Hello Reader! — Level 3

SCHOLASTIC INC.

Cartwheel
·B·O·O·K·S·®

New York Toronto London Auckland Sydney Mexico City New Delhi Hong Kong

Once there was a pumpkin.

It was large. It was very large.

The farmer was proud

of his very large pumpkin.

He was so proud of that pumpkin,

that sometimes he talked to it.

"Pumpkin," he said. "Grow!

Grow, grow, grow!"

And that's just what the pumpkin did.

It grew.

It grew and grew and grew.

Before long, it was time to pull

that pumpkin off the vine.

But the farmer could not pull it off.

The farmer pulled and pulled.

But he could not pull it off.

Now the farmer had a wife named Bell.

"Bell!" he called.

"Come help me with this pumpkin!"

So Bell came running.

Bell was big and strong.

But she could not pull
that stubborn pumpkin off the vine.

So the farmer pulled the pumpkin.

And his wife pulled the farmer.

Together, they pulled and pulled.

But they could not pull

that stubborn pumpkin off the vine.

Now the farmer and his wife Bell

had a daughter named Nell.

And Nell was big and strong.

"Nell!" called Bell.

"Be a good girl.

Come and help me

with this pumpkin."

So Nell came running.

Nell pulled and pulled.

But she could not pull
that stubborn pumpkin off
the vine.

So her father pulled the pumpkin.

And her mother pulled her father.

And Nell pulled her mother.

And together they pulled and pulled.

But they could not pull

that stubborn pumpkin off the vine.

Now the farmer and his wife Bell

and their daughter Nell

had a cow named Fifi.

And Fifi was big and strong.

"Fifi!" called Nell.

"Be a good cow.

Come and help me with this

pumpkin."

So Fifi came running.

Fifi pulled and pulled.

But she could not pull
that stubborn pumpkin off
the vine.

So the farmer pulled the pumpkin.

And his wife pulled the farmer.

And the daughter pulled her mother.

And the cow pulled the daughter.

And together, they pulled and pulled.

But they could not pull

that stubborn pumpkin off the vine.

Now the farmer and his wife Bell

and their daughter Nell

and their cow Fifi

had a dog named Pup.

And Pup was big and strong.

"Pup!" called Fifi.
"Be a good dog.
Come and help me
with this pumpkin."
So Pup came running.
Pup pulled and pulled.

But he could not pull
that stubborn pumpkin off
the vine.

So the farmer pulled the pumpkin.

And his wife pulled the farmer.

And the daughter pulled her mother.

And the cow pulled the daughter.

And the dog pulled the cow.

And together they pulled and pulled.

But still they could not pull

that stubborn pumpkin off the vine.

Now the farmer and his wife Bell

and their daughter Nell

and their cow Fifi

and their dog Pup

had a cat named Mop.

And Mop was big and strong.

"Mop!" called Pup.

"Be a good cat.

Come and help me

with this pumpkin."

So Mop came running.

Mop pulled and pulled.

But she could not pull

that stubborn pumpkin off

the vine.

So the farmer pulled the pumpkin.

And his wife pulled the farmer.

And the daughter pulled her mother.

And the cow pulled the daughter.

And the dog pulled the cow.

And the cat pulled the dog.

And together they pulled
and pulled—and pulled.
But they could not pull
that stubborn pumpkin
off the vine.

Now the farmer and his wife Bell

and their daughter Nell

and their cow Fifi

and their dog Pup

and their cat Mop

had a mouse.

The mouse's name was Henry.

Henry was not big.

And he was not strong.

"Henry!" called Mop.

"Be a good mouse.

Come and help me with this pumpkin."

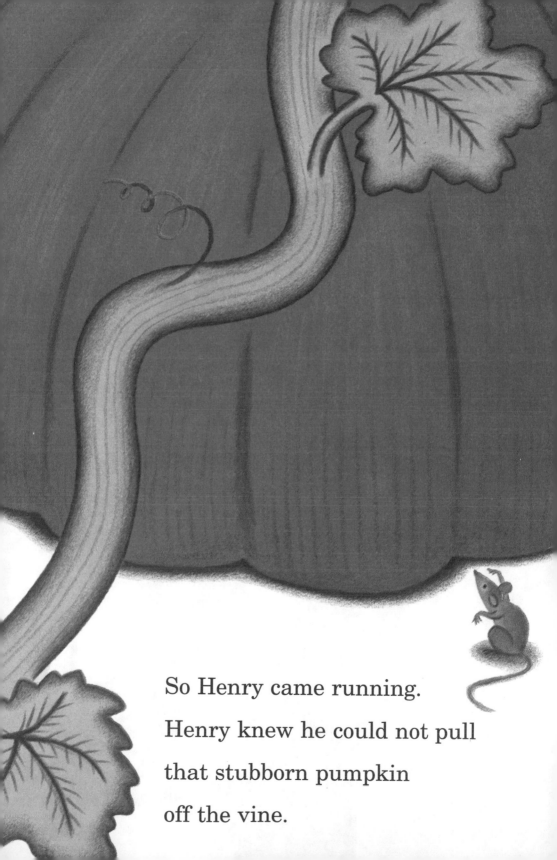

So Henry came running.
Henry knew he could not pull
that stubborn pumpkin
off the vine.

But he pulled and pulled anyway.

Then he pulled and pulled again.

Then he fell over,
huffing and puffing.

So the farmer pulled the pumpkin.

And his wife pulled the farmer.

And the daughter pulled her mother.

And the cow pulled the daughter.

And the dog pulled the cow.

And the cat pulled the dog.
And the mouse pulled the cat.

And all together, they pulled
and pulled and pulled.

Then they pulled and pulled again.
And they did not give up until…

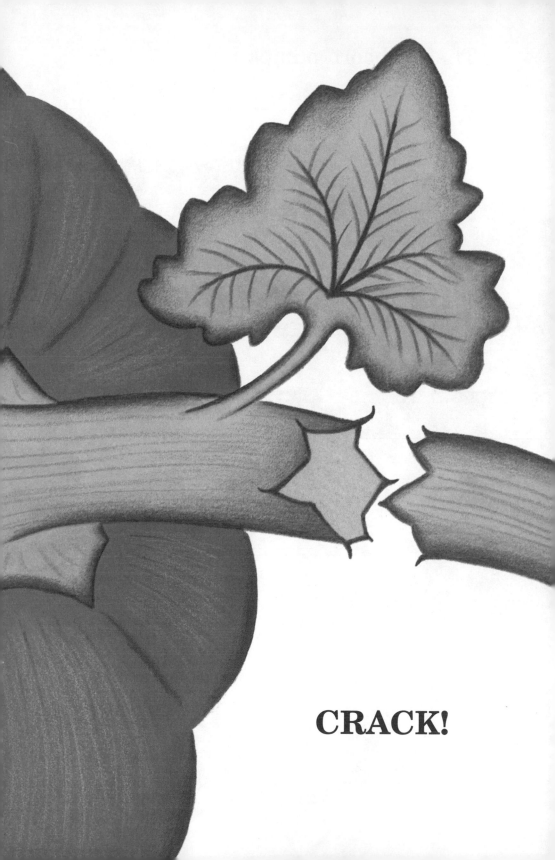

CRACK!

That stubborn pumpkin
popped off the vine!

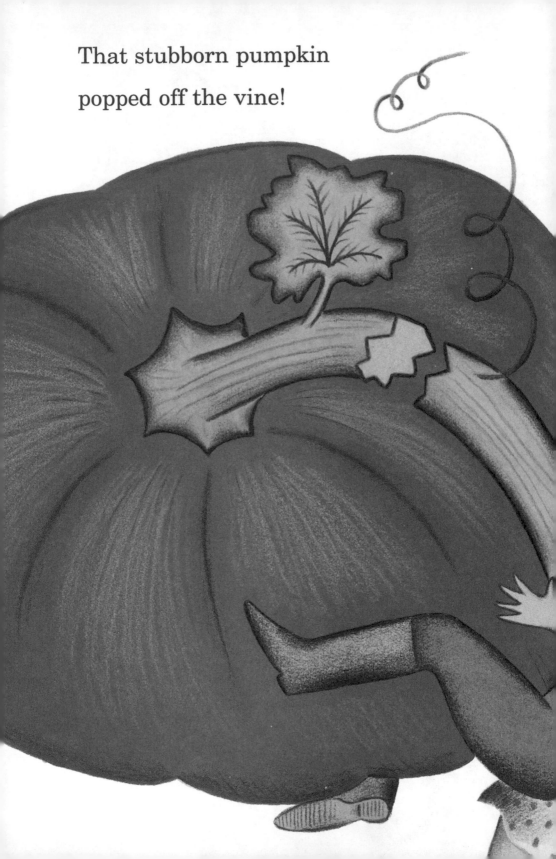

The farmer fell over,

huffing and puffing,

with the pumpkin in his arms.

And his wife fell over

with the farmer in her arms.

And their daughter fell over

with her mother in her arms.

And the cow fell over.

And the dog fell over.

And the cat fell over.

And the mouse fell over—again.

And then they all stood up.

"Hurray!" they all shouted.

And all together, they carried

that stubborn pumpkin home.

THE END